Acclaim for Colleen Coble

"Coble's atmospheric and suspenseful series launch should appeal to fans of Tracie Peterson and other authors of Christian romantic suspense."

—*Library Journal*
review of *Tidewater Inn*

"Romantically tense, but with just the right touch of danger, this cowboy love story is surprisingly clever—and pleasingly sweet."

—USAToday.com review
of *Blue Moon Promise*

"Colleen Coble will keep you glued to each page as she shows you the beauty of God's most primitive land and the dangers it hides."

—www.RomanceJunkies.com

"[An] outstanding, completely engaging tale that will have you on the edge of your seat . . . A must-have for all fans of romantic suspense!"

—TheRomanceReadersConnection.com
review of *Anathema*

"Colleen Coble lays an intricate trail in *Without a Trace* and draws the reader on like a hound with a scent."

—*Romantic Times*, 4½ stars

"Coble's historical series just keeps getting better with each entry."

"Don't ever mistake [Coble's] for the fluffy romances with a little bit of suspense. She writes solid suspense, and she ties it all together beautifully with a wonderful message."

"This book has everything I enjoy: mystery, romance, and suspense. The characters are likable, understandable, and I can relate to them."

"[M]ystery, danger, and intrigue as well as romance, love, and subtle inspiration. *The Lightkeeper's Daughter* is a 'keeper.'"

"Colleen is a master storyteller."

A
HEART'S
DISGUISE

ALSO BY COLLEEN COBLE

A
HEART'S
DISGUISE

COLLEEN
COBLE

THOMAS NELSON
Since 1798

NASHVILLE   MEXICO CITY   RIO DE JANEIRO

Published in Nashville, Tennessee, by Thomas Nelson. Thomas Nelson is a registered trademark of HarperCollins Christian Publishing, Inc.

Thomas Nelson titles may be purchased in bulk for educational, business, fund-raising, or sales promotional use. For information, please e-mail SpecialMarkets@ThomasNelson.com.

Scripture quotations are from *The Holy Bible*, King James Version.

Library of Congress Cataloging-in-Publication Data

Coble, Colleen.
   A heart's disguise / Colleen Coble.
      pages ; cm. -- (A journey of the heart ; 1)
   Summary: "In theaftermath of the Civil War, a young woman searches for her lost love at the edge of the West. The Civil War has destroyed Sarah Montgomery's marriage before it's even begun. After Sarah receives word that her fianc?, Rand Campbell, has been killed fighting for the Union, her brothers and ailing father persuade her to pledge herself to Ben Croftner--despite her strong misgivings. But when Sarah finds out that Rand is in fact alive--and that Ben Croftner knew it--she indignantly breaks off the engagement and goes in search of Rand. But Ben Croftner does not take rejection lightly--and a single woman with a sick father makes an easy target. When Sarah is abducted by her treacherous fiancé, Rand finally comes to her aid. only to reveal that he has been posted at Fort Laramie, Wyoming, and intends to take her there as his wife. But could Sarah leave her dying father's side for the love of her life? And what plans are forming in the jealous heart of Ben Croftner?"-- Provided by publisher.
   ISBN 978-0-529-10341-3 (softcover)
   1. Triangles (Interpersonal relations)--Fiction. 2. Man-woman relationships--Fiction. 3. United States--History--Civil War, 1861-1865--Fiction. I. Title.
   PS3553.O2285H43 2015
   813'.54--dc23
                                    2014037044

Printed in the United States of America
15 16 17 18 19 RRD 6 5 4 3 2 1

In memory of my brother Randy Rhoads, who taught me to love the mountains of Wyoming, and my grandparents Everett and Eileen Everroad, who loved me unconditionally. May you walk those heavenly mountains with joy.

A Letter from the Author

―――――――――――――― ⁘ ――――――――――――――

Dear Reader,

  I can't tell you how excited I am to share this story with you! It's the first series I ever wrote, and it will always be special to me because writing was how I dealt with my brother Randy's death. You'll see a piece of my dear brother in Rand's character throughout this series. These four books were originally titled *Where Leads the Heart* and *Plains of Promise*. They haven't been available in print form for nearly ten years, so I'm thrilled to share them with you.

―――――――――――――― ⁘ ――――――――――――――

When my brother Randy was killed in a freak lightning accident, I went to Wyoming to see where he had lived. Standing on the parade ground at Fort Laramie, the idea for the first book dropped into my head. I went home excited to write it. It took a year to write, and I thought for sure there would be a bidding war on it! :) Not so much. It took six more years for a publisher to pick it up. But the wait was worth it!

This series seemed a good one to break up into a serialization model to introduce readers to my work. Even in my early stories, I had to have villains and danger lurking around the corner. :) I hope you enjoy this trip back in time with me.

E-mail me at colleen@colleencoble.com and let me know what you think!

Love,
Colleen

ONE

❧

Wabash, Indiana, October 1865

Autumn's chill matched Sarah Montgomery's heart. The war had taken so much from her, and it seemed impossible for life to ever get to a hopeful place. The scent of turning leaves lingered in the air as she sat on a porch rocking chair beside her father, who was huddled in a blanket. Her bustle bunched under her uncomfortably, but she wanted to be close to her ill father for as long as possible before Ben arrived.

The sun lingered on the horizon, casting rays of gold and red across the Indiana sky. In the distance, she could see the silhouettes of the workers in the field as they tossed the last of the ears of corn into the wagon behind the horses.

"Bed sounds better than a party." She stifled a yawn. "I'm getting tired of dances every night, though I can't begrudge everyone's revelry." The Union was preserved, but the price had been so high. Scarcely a family in the county had been spared the loss of a loved one.

Her father coughed and tugged the blanket higher on his chest. "I'm glad you're beginning to enjoy life again. Rand wouldn't want you to grieve."

"No. No, he wouldn't." But what no one seemed to understand was that her fiancé's death in the war had left a hole that couldn't be filled. Not ever.

His cold hand clamped down on her wrist. "I need to see you settled before I die, Sarah."

She flinched. "Don't talk like that, Papa." She couldn't bear to lose him—not when she'd already lost so much.

He rubbed his forehead. "You heard the doctor as plainly as I did last week. This old ticker isn't going to hold out much longer. I want you to marry Ben Croftner. He'll be a good husband to you."

Sarah wanted to bolt from the porch, to hide herself in the dusty golden stalks and forget her father's request. "Ben isn't Rand. I don't think I can do it."

"Rand is never coming back, honey. Do you want to live here in this house with Wade the rest of your life?"

She looked down at the bowl of corn in her hands. "No."

Her older brother thought he always knew best, and the two of them had never gotten along. "What about Joel?" She'd raised her eight-year-old brother from infancy when their mother died in childbirth. Any future she might plan had to include Joel.

"He should go with you. Wade is too hard on him, and he wouldn't do well without you." Her father coughed away a wheeze.

She couldn't believe she was actually thinking about it, but what other choice did she have? She liked Ben well enough. He had a nice home along the Wabash River, and he was always kind to Joel.

"I'll think about it," she said as Ben's carriage came into view.

Ben swung Sarah around the dance floor past hay bales, bridles, and plows. The fiddle and the melody lifted her spirits, dampened by so much death and heartache. Women in hoop skirts and men in top hats had thrown off the heartache of the War Between the States tonight as they dipped and swayed on the barn floor. The food shortages had eased some, and the aroma of apple pie—a scarcity with the lack of sugar—wafted through the space.

Ben was such a fine dancer, strong and graceful in a way that made her feel she could float across the floor in his arms. He grinned down at her, sensing perhaps that she was beginning to enjoy herself just a little, for once.

Ben tightened his grip around her waist possessively. "Come outside a minute, would you, Sarah? I want to talk to you." His smile was warm, but his firm voice brooked no objection. She let him lead her toward the big sliding door of the barn, beyond wooden tables piled high with pumpkin rolls and pies of every imaginable flavor, past the seated older women who watched their exit with wistful smiles.

As Ben led her into the cool of the evening, Sarah's weariness gave way to a rising dread. After her father's request before the dance, she suspected Ben had already mentioned his intentions to her family. She wasn't ready.

Her steps faltered as she hung back. "Wait, Ben. Let me get my shawl." Her hands shaking, she took her blue shawl from a peg on the wall and wrapped it around her shoulders.

"Come on, Sarah." His face purposeful and his voice impatient, Ben tugged on her arm and drew her outside.

The full moon shone down on them, but the most light came from the lanterns strung around the graying barn and through the muddy yard. The lights dipped and swayed like fireflies in the light breeze. The air was moist and tangy, a mixture of ripening grain and the smoke from a bonfire in the adjoining field. The October night had a slight chill, and Sarah pulled her shawl more closely about her shoulders.

Ben pulled Sarah down onto a bench away from several other couples watching the bonfire shoot sparks high into the darkening sky. "It's time we talked about our future, Sarah." He hesitated as if gauging her reaction. "I want to marry you. You know how I've felt about you for years, and now that Rand's gone—well, I hope you'll consider me."

Sarah raised a trembling hand to her throat and felt her pulse fluttering under her fingertips. How did she tell him Rand still occupied her heart? That she would never love anyone again? She swallowed hard, but the words stuck in her throat.

Did she have the obligation to make others happy when it was in her power? She owed it to Papa to get her life settled. How could she refuse to do whatever it took to ease her father's worries? And besides, what else did the future hold except to be someone's wife? Like her father had said, she didn't want to live with Wade the rest of her life.

She stared up into Ben's earnest face. "What about Joel? I can't go anywhere without him."

"I know that, honey. He's more like your own boy than your brother. We have plenty of bedrooms. I hope to fill the rest of them with babies Joel can be a big brother to."

His words eased the ache in her heart somewhat. Didn't Joel deserve a more normal life too? Ben was a good man, a successful man. He'd make sure she and

Joel never wanted for anything. What more could she really hope for? "All right. I'll marry you."

Ben smiled in spite of her lackluster response. "I'm so glad, my dear. You won't be sorry."

Her stomach sank as she twisted her icy hands in the folds of her skirt. *I already am.*

"Shall we go announce our good news?" Without waiting for her answer, he drew her up and tucked her hand into the crook of his elbow. "Your family will be so pleased."

She pushed her shoulders back and held her head erect as they walked into the barn. She could do this, for her family. For her father and brothers.

Ben pulled her with him to the front of the room and waved his hands. "Ladies and gentlemen, may I have your attention?"

The music stopped with a last, dying squeal of the fiddle, and flushed couples stared back at them. Her cheeks burned and Sarah took a deep, calming breath. She caught her dear friend Amelia's stricken look and nodded encouragingly.

Sarah glanced up at Ben. He was so good-looking, though in a different way than Rand had been. Ben's hair was blond, almost white, and he had gray eyes the color of the Wabash River on a stormy day. He had a self-confident air, and his charm smoothed most obstacles he encountered. Like her father had said, she would never want for anything as Ben's wife. *Except for love.*

Ben dropped a possessive arm around her shoulders. "You all know how long I've tried to get Sarah to agree to be my wife."

"I always thought she showed a lot of sense," called Jason Maxwell from up in the haymow, where a group of young men had been playing checkers. Some adolescent boys who'd been watching the game hooted with laughter. "The prettiest girl in town ought to be able to do better than you."

Ben laughed, too, but there was little humor in his eyes. "Well, you can all congratulate me—she finally gave in! You're all invited to the wedding—and it'll be a humdinger!"

Friends and neighbors crowded around quickly to congratulate them, and Sarah was hugged and kissed as she fought to keep her smile from slipping. Wade grinned smugly as he shook Ben's hand.

Joel came over for a quick embrace. "What about me?"

She was the only one who heard his whisper, and

she pulled him close. "Ben says you can live with us. It will be like a real home, honey. You'll see. And you can go see Papa anytime you like. We'll live close."

His smile came then, and he released his tight grip on her. Over his shoulder, she saw the two Campbell boys, Rand's brothers, making their way away from the party. What must they think of her? When Joel turned to speak to Ben, she ducked away quietly and hurried to intercept them.

They stopped beside the heavily laden tables to wait for her. Before she could say a word, Jacob took her hand in his, his dark eyes, so like his older brother's, sad in spite of his smile. "No need to worry about us, Sarah. We saw this coming. Besides, Rand wouldn't want you to grieve forever. We just want you to be happy. Right, Shane?"

The youngest Campbell pushed his blond hair out of his face and turned sober blue eyes on her. "Right. The only thing is—" He hesitated and looked from Jacob to Sarah. "What if Rand's not really dead?"

Sarah gasped. "What on earth do you mean?" There was a faint flutter of hope in her chest. Did they know something they hadn't told her? Shane held his tongue. "What does he mean, Jacob?" she asked.

"Rand is dead. Ben saw his body in Andersonville. Father got official notification from the army. And his name was on the list in the newspaper."

"But we never got his body or his things." Shane's chin jutted out. "There could still be some mistake. Maybe he was wounded real bad. Maybe Ben was wrong."

Jacob frowned at his brother. "Shane, that's enough. It's been over a year since he was reported dead. Don't you think Rand would have written? Or the army would have contacted us? It's no wonder we didn't get his body back or his things. The casualties were too overwhelming. Thousands were buried in unmarked graves. Both Union and Rebs. I know—I was there at the Battle of Chickamauga. We don't know how he died, but I have no doubt he's gone. You have to face the truth, Shane."

Shane's eyes shone with unshed tears, and Sarah fought tears of her own. She didn't think she would ever get used to the reality of Rand's death, but she understood why Jacob was being so brutal. Shane couldn't begin to heal until he accepted it. Just as she was finally beginning to accept it.

Jacob put a comforting arm around Shane's

shoulders as tears trickled down the youngster's cheeks. "I'm sorry, Sarah. I had no idea such a notion was brewing in that brain of his. Forget what he said and just be happy." He reached out and touched her cheek. "Ben's a lucky guy. But remember, whatever happens, you'll always be a part of our family too."

"Thank you, Jacob. I'll remember," she whispered as she watched them thread their way through the throng.

There was a soft touch on her arm, and she whirled, thinking it was Ben, that he would see her tears. But it was just Amelia, her blue eyes anxious. "You're crying. Are you all right?"

"Oh yes. It's just those Campbell boys. They're so sweet . . ."

Amelia laughed. "I am awfully fond of Jacob."

"Good thing you're marrying him then, isn't it?" The two friends laughed and hugged. Amelia held Sarah at arm's length and leveled her gaze. "Are you being honest with me? You're not crying about Ben's announcement?"

"No, of course not," Sarah objected, a little more strenuously than she meant to. "I'm thrilled!"

"Now I know you're lying to me."

"I know you don't approve of Ben, but this is really for the best. Wade says . . ."

"Wade says? When did Wade ever say a sensible thing in his life? Just tell me this: Can you look me in the eyes and tell me you love Ben?"

Sarah pressed her lips together. Amelia always cut right through to the heart of the matter. "Amelia, I know you mean well, but that question gets us nowhere. I have to marry soon or I'll die a spinster in Wade's home." She shuddered. "And Ben loves me." The excuses sounded weak, even to her own ears. "It may not be the life I'd dreamed of or hoped for, but Ben can provide a good life for me."

Amelia hesitated, eyeing Sarah. "You know I want that for you. You deserve that and more. But why Ben? I don't think you love him."

"I like him well enough. Since he got back from the war, he's about the most popular man to walk the streets of Wabash." Sarah nodded toward the cluster of young ladies hovering around Ben in the middle of the floor. "I know a couple of girls who would give anything to be in my shoes. Be happy for me, Amelia. Please? Will you stand up for me and be my bridesmaid?"

Amelia sighed. "Of course I will, if we're still here. Jacob's leave is almost over. He has to report for duty at Fort Laramie soon. When is the wedding?"

"We haven't set a date yet, but don't worry—you'll still be the first bride." Sarah didn't know how she could stand to be separated from her best friend. From across the barn, Ben motioned for her to join him. "I've got to go, but we'll get together tomorrow and make some plans. Okay?" She hurried off, pinning her smile back on.

By the time all the well-wishing and hugging were over, the rest of Sarah's family had left to go home. She'd hoped they'd all be in bed by the time Ben dropped her off.

At Sarah's house, a dim light still shone through the parlor window's lace curtains as Ben helped her down from the buggy. The window was open, and she could smell the aroma of fresh-brewed coffee. Evidently no one was going to bed anytime soon.

He leaned down to kiss her. "You've made me very happy tonight, my dear."

She flinched a bit as his lips grazed her cheek. She'd better get used to it. Ben grasped her waist and started to pull her closer. In spite of her resolve, Sarah quickly pulled away from his grip. "I'd better go in. My father is waiting up. I'll see you tomorrow?"

She rushed up the stairs without waiting for a reply, her heart lightening a bit with every step. When she walked onto the wide front porch, she glanced back. Ben watched her with an unsmiling stare. Had she upset him?

She dragged her eyes from his gaze and called out a cheerful "Good night," hoping she'd misread his look. Weary from the long night, she pushed herself through the front door.

The murmur of voices echoed from the parlor. She hung her shawl on a hook and walked into the room. The thick rug muffled her footsteps, but Wade looked up from the overstuffed chintz chair beside the fireplace. Her father lay on the matching sofa, his breathing labored and his face pale in the dying light from the fireplace.

She quickly knelt at his side. "Papa, are you all right? Should I call Doc Seth?"

"No, no. I'm fine. Just tired." His breathing seemed

to ease as he took her hand and drew her into an embrace. "You remind me so much of your mama the first time I met her." He closed his eyes and grimaced. "I'm going to miss you when you go. It will be almost like losing her again."

Wade's wife came into the parlor carrying a tray laden with cups of steaming coffee. Sarah reached for her sister-in-law's burden. "Here, Rachel. Let me take that. It's much too heavy for you in your condition." Sarah eyed the gentle bulge under Rachel's skirt.

Rachel handed it over with a tired smile of thanks and a glance at her husband.

Wade took a cup of coffee. "Congratulations, Sarah. Ben is quite a catch. Just see you don't forget your family when you're rich."

Was money all he ever thought about? Sarah bit back an angry retort. She didn't want to upset her father. "Why would you say such a thing? You know money isn't important to me."

Wade laughed. "It's all right. You'll see soon enough the difference money makes in this world. Besides, I always thought you could do better than Campbell."

Sarah curled her fingers into her palms and inhaled

to fire back a comment. Wade would never listen to her anyway.

Her father's tender gaze lingered on her. "You were only eleven when your mama died, much too young to take over the household and your new brother the way you did." He wiped a shaking hand across his brow, beaded with drops of sweat. "But I just was so blinded by my own grief, I wasn't thinking clearly. All these years you've managed our home like it was your own. It's time for you to leave here and have your own life, your own home."

Wade slammed his coffee cup down on the table, and some of it sloshed onto the polished walnut surface. "Sure, Sarah played house, but I was always out in the fields working my fingers to the bone to support this family. If not for my hard work, this place would have gone on the auction block long ago. You never seem to remember we all worked together."

His father looked up at him. "You're right, son. I don't tell you often enough how grateful I am that you shouldered the responsibility." He sat up and swung his legs off the couch. "You get on up to bed now. That's where I'm headed."

At least his voice seemed stronger.

Her father laid a gentle hand on her arm. "Why don't you go on up to bed? You can tell us all about your plans tomorrow."

Her anger faded, and she gave a weary nod. It didn't do any good to argue with Wade anyway. He had never liked Rand, probably because he was one of the few people Wade couldn't intimidate. She kissed her father and bid them all good night, then walked upstairs, running her hand along the smooth oak banister. She looked back down into the entryway as she thought about her father's words. She was going to miss this place.

Once in the sanctuary of her room, she stepped out of her hoopskirt and crinoline and struggled with the buttons on her dress. She looked around her bedroom. She'd miss this house, this large room furnished with dainty white furniture stenciled with pink. A lacy coverlet topped the feather bed, and dozens of pastel pillows offered a plump, safe haven to curl up and read. Rand had made the bed for their wedding before he went off to war, and it wouldn't be appropriate to take it with her to Ben's. The very thought was hideous.

She took the pins from her long hair and let it fall

to her shoulders, then pulled her nightgown over her head. She smoothed the two braids loose, then ran her brush through the tresses before rebraiding it in one long plait.

The smooth sheets welcomed her, and she pulled her feather comforter up to her chin. She was filled with a strange foreboding as Shane's words came back to her. *"What if Rand's not really dead?"* She'd indulged in such daydreams in the first months after his death. But tonight the idea followed her into her dreams.

TWO

~~~

After a long day of negotiating with the railroad for some land he owned, Ben approached the stately brick two-story with a profound sense of pride. Everything he wanted was within his grasp. He swung off his fine quarter horse and led him into the barn, calling for the stable boy.

Who would have thought that Ben Croftner, son of the good-for-nothing drifter Max Croftner, would pull himself up by his own bootstraps out of the dirt and live in a house that was the envy of everyone in

Wabash—and Indiana, for that matter? He'd done what he had to do to get to the top. There had been much opportunity since the war, and he discovered he had an aptitude for exploiting it. He'd made a fortune the last six months.

And now Sarah Montgomery was finally his. Beautiful Sarah with her mesmerizing green eyes and red-gold hair. He'd be the envy of the men in town, few though they were.

He wiped his dusty shoes on the rug by the door, then stepped into the elegantly appointed front parlor. Velvet drapes, fine walnut tables and Dresden figurines, a plush rug imported from France, and an overstuffed horsehair sofa and chair. He frowned as he saw the figure on the sofa. Too bad he couldn't just leave his family behind the same way he'd left his old life.

Labe jumped up from the sofa, clutching an envelope. "I'm not going to do it anymore, Ben." His voice quivered as he handed over the envelope. "My boss at the post office almost caught me this time. And I'm not going to jail for nobody. Not even you."

Ben patted Labe's shoulder. "Don't worry, little brother. Sarah finally gave in last night. By the time the next letter comes, she'll be my wife."

Labe's mouth dropped open. "Congratulations, then. I never thought you'd really pull it off. When you came back from the war with this crazy scheme, I thought fighting them Rebs had made you loco."

Ben laughed as he sank into the plushness of the high-backed chair and took off his sweat-stained Stetson and wiped his face. Labe wasn't the first to underestimate his ambition. "Like I said, it's all over. Now all you have to do is keep your mouth shut."

He looked at the envelope in his lap. "I suppose I should read what this says." Ben ripped open the top and took out the single sheet of paper. "Won't Mr. High and Mighty Rand Campbell be surprised when he finds his beloved Sarah is married to me!"

He settled more comfortably in his chair and scanned the sprawling lines. His smile faded and a scowl twisted his face. He ripped the page to shreds, tossed them onto the fire burning in the grate, and stood.

"What is it, Ben?"

"Rand's coming home. But no matter. He'll be too late." He strode out the door without another word to Labe.

He flung the harness over his horse's still-damp

neck and hitched up the buggy. As he flicked the buggy whip over the horse's head and headed toward the Montgomery farm, he pressed his lips together with determination. He hadn't kept up a charade for five months to lose Sarah now.

He'd been so careful, so patient, telling her how he'd found Rand in the prison camp and got him to the hospital, only for him to die there. And Rand *should* have died. He'd been just a shell of a man with his skin stretched over his bones when he was finally liberated from Andersonville. It was the most hideous thing Ben had ever seen. But he had rallied, much to Ben's dismay. He really hadn't expected Rand to recuperate as fast as he had, and now he threatened to spoil all Ben's carefully laid plans. Ben couldn't let that happen. He wouldn't.

Sarah was sweeping the front porch when Ben stepped down out of the buggy. She forced herself to relax and lift a hand in greeting when he approached. How good-looking he was. His blond hair just curled over his collar, and his gray eyes were gentle and tender, dispelling her misgivings from the night before. She was doing the right thing.

Ben bounded up the steps with a smile and took her hand. "How's my lovely lady today?"

She smiled up at him. "I'm getting behind in my housework. Everyone has been stopping by to congratulate me. News travels fast."

"Especially good news." He guided her down onto the porch steps and sat beside her. "I was talking to Labe, and he was saying how good it would be to have a real woman doing for us once you and I are married. We haven't decided on a date yet, but I was hoping to make it on my birthday next weekend. Could you be ready?"

"But, Ben, that's only eight days." Panic rose in her throat, and she tried to keep the dismay out of her face as she stared at him. "There's such a lot to do."

"You can be ready, I'm sure, if you really want to be." A note of impatience crept into his voice. "Don't you think you've made me wait long enough?"

"But I have to make my dress. And—"

"I surely don't care what you wear. Your Sunday dress will do just fine."

She lowered her eyes. Why did he always make

her feel so guilty, so indebted to him? "I can be ready. Would you like some iced tea?"

"No, I have a meeting in town. I'll see you tonight."

She allowed his hug, then, with something that felt like relief, watched him ride away. What difference did it really make anyway? One date was as good as another if she was really going to go through with it. And besides, if she wanted Amelia to be her bridesmaid, they'd have to wed before Amelia and Jacob left for Fort Laramie.

Dinner was yet to be made, but Sarah untied her apron and started toward the McCallister farm. She needed to see her friend. She paused at the knoll overlooking Amelia's home. The hills were green with giant oak and maple trees. Several milk cows grazed on the thick, lush grass under a bowl of blue sky. Doctor Seth and his family still lived in the log home he'd built when he first arrived twenty years ago. With his thriving practice, he could well afford an elaborate home in town. But she was glad the McCallisters had never moved. It was her second home, and she ran over the meadow that separated the two properties.

The house had been added on to over the years and now sprawled carelessly in several directions. Their two families had been close ever since Sarah could remember. At one time there was hope that Amelia would marry Wade, but she lost interest as Wade grew to manhood and became the arrogant, self-righteous boor he was. Now Amelia had eyes for no other man but Jacob Campbell.

Amelia was on the wide front porch, churning butter. She greeted Sarah with a smile, her face flushed with exertion. "I was just coming to see you as soon as I was finished." Tendrils of dark hair clung in curls around her face. "I have some ideas for the wedding." Her welcoming smile faded. "What's wrong?"

"I don't know what to do." Sarah launched into an explanation of Ben's plans.

Amelia started shaking her head before Sarah finished. "Eight days! That isn't enough time to get everything ready."

"I know! I tried to tell him that, but he wouldn't listen. He wants to be married on his birthday." Sarah slumped down onto a step. "And I guess it's the least I can do after all I've put him through these past five months. You know how patient he's been . . ." Her voice faltered when she saw the skeptical look Amelia threw her way, and Sarah realized how ridiculous she sounded. "Besides, if we wait until after your wedding, you might have to leave before mine."

"I suppose you're right," Amelia said slowly. "But I've never understood why you think you owe Ben anything. He hasn't done anything special for you." She came to sit next to Sarah on the step. "You say Ben loves you. I'm sure that's true. Who wouldn't? But do you really know his heart, Sarah? Does he know you don't love him?"

"Don't start, Amelia. Please."

Amelia recoiled at her uncharacteristic harshness.

"I'm sorry." Sarah hugged her friend. "It's just that I have to go through with it. Papa wants to see me settled before . . ." She bit her lip. "And besides"— she gave Amelia a wink—"I was thinking how nice it will be to get away from Wade and his constant disapproval."

Amelia smiled and blinked away her tears. "He just needs the Lord in his life."

Sarah was a little envious of her friend's faith. No matter what happened, Amelia seemed to trust God. She never had a bad word to say about anyone.

That's why her attitude toward Ben was so perplexing. But really, this was for the best if Amelia could just see it. Sarah would make a fresh start with Ben, and as the years passed and she had children to occupy her time, maybe the pain in her heart would ease.

The next few days sped by as Sarah threw herself into wedding preparations. Papa had bought her a Singer treadle sewing machine. Her dress, even with its yards and yards of soft, creamy lace, quickly took shape under its whirring needle. She fell into bed each night too exhausted to think or even to dream.

Friday afternoon she sat back and massaged her aching neck thankfully. It was finally finished. She stared out the living room window at the weeping willows swaying along the riverbank. The soft breeze, laden with the rich scent of the Wabash River, blew through the sheer curtains and caressed her hot face.

A memory of walking hand in hand with Rand along the river's edge hit her, and she clutched her skirt, anguish burning in her belly. Why couldn't she stop thinking about him? She'd be Mrs. Ben Croftner in a few days. Then maybe all the ghosts would be laid to rest.

She jumped as the knocker on the front door clattered. When she opened the door, Pastor Aaron Stevens stood on the porch, turning his hat in his hands. "Pastor. We didn't expect you. I believe Wade and Rachel have gone out for a bit and Father is resting. But won't you come in?"

He followed her into the parlor. "I was out calling on the new family by the river, the Longs, and just thought I'd stop in and see how you're doing."

She pointed to the heap of cream material on the sewing machine. "I just finished my dress."

"Are you all right, Sarah? You look . . ." He hesitated as he sat on the sofa. "Well, troubled. Not quite the picture of a joyous bride-to-be I expected."

Pastor always seemed able to sense her moods in a strange way. She sighed and nodded. "I guess I am troubled. More than I've admitted to anyone else. And I don't *want* to be! This is for the best—I'm sure of it."

"I detect some trepidation in your manner. Are you trying to convince me or yourself?" Pastor Stevens pushed his heavy black hair away from his forehead. "Have you prayed about it?"

Sarah lifted her chin mutinously. "Not really. And

I know you're going to say I should. But God didn't seem to be listening all those months when I prayed for Rand's safety." She looked down at her hands.

Pastor Stevens frowned as he leaned forward. "I had a feeling you blamed God for Rand's death. I'm glad you're finally admitting it." He took her hand, his blue eyes warm with concern and compassion. "Sarah, please listen to me. It's hard, I know, but we can't always see God's plan in our lives. I remember when I was a little boy, lying on the floor at my grandmother's feet. She was doing some embroidery work, and I looked up at the underside of the hoop. The yarn was all tangled and gnarled. A real mess. But when I climbed up beside her and looked down at what she was working on, it was a beautiful garden. That's the way our lives are. We're looking at the picture from underneath, but God is working out a specific plan from above."

"No plan could be right without Rand in it. I don't care whose it is!" She didn't care if the words shocked her pastor. It was how she really felt. If God really loved her, he wouldn't let her go through this heartache.

Pastor Stevens got up and knelt beside Sarah's

chair. "God loves you, Sarah. He didn't promise we'd never have trouble or heartache. In fact, the Bible tells us we will. But he's given us his Word to go with us every step of the way. Can't you just trust him like you used to? I remember the old Sarah and how she believed God for every little thing in her life. Wouldn't you like to be that same young woman again?"

"I just can't!" She stood and moved to the window, her back to the pastor. "Maybe someday when the wounds aren't still so fresh, I'll be able to trust him like I should. But nothing has turned out like I expected. Every time I see the knoll on the other side of the woods, I'm reminded of the spot where Rand and I meant to build our home. Everywhere I look are reminders of how my life is in shambles."

She turned abruptly. "If you don't mind, Pastor, I have a lot of things to finish up." She knew she sounded rude, but she just couldn't talk about it anymore. It hurt too much.

He stood with reluctance, frustration etched on his face. "If you need to talk, you know where to find me. Please pray about this before you go through with it, Sarah."

She didn't answer him, and he left after gazing at

her for a moment. She breathed a sigh of relief when she heard the front door shut. She pushed away a stab of guilt as she went to the kitchen to start supper. She'd chosen her course, and she'd stick with it.

THREE

The train shrieked a warning of imminent arrival, and Rand Campbell jerked awake, his heart pounding. He licked dry lips—how he'd love a drink of his ma's iced tea. The thought of sun tea brewing in a glass jug on the back step at home caused a fresh wave of homesickness to wash over him. It wouldn't be long, though.

Then the fear he'd tried to keep at bay for the past three days flooded back. What would he find at home? He'd passed mile after mile of war-ravaged scenes.

Homes burned to the ground, fences torn down, hopeless looks on the faces of women and children. What if he arrived and found his home gone and his family missing? And Sarah. What if she was dead? What if she didn't wait for him? He pushed the thought away impatiently. His Sarah would wait no matter what. But then why didn't she write? Why hadn't his mother written? The unanswered questions made him feel sick.

The train whistle blew again, and he peered out the soot-streaked window. He was almost home. Eagerly, he scanned the rolling pastures. There was the Johnson place looking as neat and well-tended as usual. The Larsen farm looked unharmed. The train slowed as it began its descent into the valley. Through clearings in the lush canopy of glowing leaves, he could see the town just beyond.

The town of Wabash nestled between two steep hills, with the courthouse on the far hill overlooking the sprawling brick and wood buildings clustered neatly below it. He drank in the familiar buildings and the glimmer of water that ran in front of the town like a silver ribbon. During the heyday of the Wabash-Erie Canals, the river bustled with boats of all types and sizes, but since the railroad came, the

34

canal traffic slacked off, and the river once again resumed its placid course.

Hungrily he watched for a familiar face. But the streets and boardwalks were almost deserted. The few people hurrying along were strangers, mostly women. So many men lost their lives in the war.

But the town looked just the same. There was Beitman & Wolf's. And Martha's Millinery, her fly-speckled window crowded with bonnets. Several old-timers in bib overalls lounged outside Lengel's Gun Shop.

Did the younger members of town still patronize the Red Onion Saloon? He grinned at a memory of the last ruckus he'd gotten into at the saloon, much to his grandma's dismay. She was always quoting Proverbs to him after an escapade at the Red Onion.

Those Bible verses he'd memorized at her knee were one of the things that got him through the horror of prison camp. Between starvation, dysentery, and murderous gangs, he'd watched a third of the men in camp die. He didn't really understand some of the verses very well, but they were somehow comforting. Maybe when his life settled down a little, he could study the Scriptures for himself.

His smile faded. The war had changed him and not for the better. Was there a way to get past the horrors he'd seen? He pushed his grandmother's memory away and gazed out the window intently.

The train gave one final, wheezing bellow, then came to a shuddering stop under the overhang of the depot. Rand took a deep breath and stood, pulling his haversack out from under his seat. Wouldn't it be grand if Pa or Jacob were in town? No chance of that, though. For one thing, he was here a good week earlier than he'd written he'd be. Lot more likely to find them in the field on the way home, if Jacob was even here. *And if he survived the war.*

His weak leg, injured by a bayonet, gave out as he stepped down, and he fell into an elderly, stooped man. "Why, I-I cain't believe it! Rand Campbell, is it really you?" Liam Murphy had worked at the train station for as long as Rand could remember. He grabbed Rand by the shoulders and peered into his face.

His hair was even more grizzled than Rand remembered, and his breath stank of garlic. Rand suppressed a grin. Liam's wife believed in garlic's medicinal qualities, so most folks steered clear of her specialties at the church picnics. "It's me all right, Liam."

"Rand," the old man gasped again before enfolding him in a bear hug. "We heard you was dead, boy."

Rand hugged him back until his words penetrated, then drew back in shock. "What do you mean, dead? I wrote my folks and Sarah every few weeks. I've been in the hospital in Washington, D.C."

Liam pulled a filthy handkerchief from his pocket and wiped his face with a shaking hand. "Wait till Myra hears 'bout this!" He put the dirty cloth back in his pocket. "Don't know nothing about no letters. No one here got no letters, I'm sure. Your folks been grieving themselves to death over you. Had a memorial service at church for you last spring, and I ain't never seen so many people at one of them things." He stared in Rand's puzzled face. "I'm telling you—we all thought you was dead!"

Rand felt like he'd been punched in the stomach. He couldn't catch his breath. How could something like this have happened? "I-I sent a letter with Ben Croftner to give to Sarah," he stammered. "Didn't he make it back here?"

A look of surprise and something else Rand couldn't identify flickered across Liam's face. "Yeah, he got back—let's see. Must be pert near five months ago." He paused and glanced at Rand. "But he didn't say nothing about no letter."

Something was odd in Liam's manner. "What aren't you telling me?" He fixed his eyes on the old porter's face.

The man flushed. "Well, now—I-I guess you have to hear it sooner or later," he stammered. "Ben's supposed to marry Sarah tomorrow. Right after church. Whole town's been invited. Ben's been strutting around all important-like."

The strength left Rand's knees, and he sat on the passenger bench outside the depot. The implications of what Liam said began to sink in, along with the bitter knowledge of Ben's betrayal. "I thought he was my friend. He let her go on thinking I was dead." He stood and slung his haversack over one broad shoulder, then turned south and strode off without saying good-bye to Liam, his slight limp more pronounced because of his fatigue.

Rand clamped down on the rage that was building in him. How could Ben do such a thing? And Sarah. How could she be so fickle? Why, he must have been declared dead only a few months before she took up with Croftner! Was that all the time she mourned someone she was supposed to love? His emotions felt raw, and he just couldn't seem to make any sense out of it.

By the time he made his way to the livery stable, paid for a horse, and swung up into the saddle, he was shaking with fury. He patted the mare's neck and set off toward home.

Being astride a horse again for the first time in a year cleared his thoughts, and he was more in control of his emotions by the time he pulled the mare off the road and headed up the deeply rutted track that followed the river. To gather his thoughts, he let the horse graze in the knee-high grass along the dirt track. He'd have Shane return the rental horse to the livery. His own horse, Ranger, would be glad to see him. He sat a moment and gazed out at Campbell land. The fields were tawny with drying corn. Harvest would be in a few weeks.

He turned the horse's head and urged her up onto the road again. They rounded the corner, and his heart quickened as the white two-story home on the hill overlooking the river came into view. Home. How he'd longed for this moment.

He pulled the horse up sharply. Should he go home first or see Sarah and demand an explanation? He could just see the roof of the large Montgomery house over the next rise. He let the horse prance on the path for a moment as he decided what to do.

No. He dug his heels into the mare's flank and turned up the Campbell lane. His family first. At least they'd mourned for him.

By the time he reached the front yard, his heart pounded and his palms were slick with sweat. A nagging headache persisted just behind his eyes. He pulled his horse to a stop and dismounted, a little disappointed no one was outside. He guided the horse to the shade of a big oak tree and tied her where she could reach the grass.

As he approached the back door, through the window he could see his mother washing dishes. A wave of love welled up in him as he saw the new gray in her hair and the fine web of wrinkles at her eyes. He breathed in the familiar scent of apple pie baking in the oven as he quietly opened the door.

His mother's back was to him, and he watched her a moment as she picked up a dish and proceeded to wash it. "I think I heard a horse," she said to the little brown dog lying on the rug by her feet. "Probably one of the menfolk home."

The little dog pricked her ears and whined as she

looked toward the door. His mother dipped the soapy plate in the pan of rinse water and laid it to drain on the wooden chopping block beside her.

Rand let the screen door bang behind him, but she didn't turn. "Don't bang the door," she said. Jody yipped and launched herself in a frenzy toward the door. His mother wiped her soapy hands on her apron and turned. Her eyes went wide as her gaze swept over him, then returned to lock with his.

"Ma." Rand knelt and picked up the little dog as he stared at his mother.

She froze, and Rand saw one emotion after another chase across her face. Uncertainty, disbelief, hope. She clutched her hands in the folds of her apron.

"Ma, I'm home." Rand patted Jody and laughed as the dog wriggled in his arms and licked his face joyously.

Her mouth opened, but no sound emerged as she stared at him.

"It's me, Ma."

"Rand?" she whispered as she took a faltering step toward him. "Rand!" With a noise something between a cry and a croak, she threw herself into his arms as the tears started down her cheeks.

Rand inhaled the aroma of her sachet, something

sweet with a rose scent. He struggled not to let the moisture burning his eyes slide down his cheeks. Home. He was finally home.

"Let me look at you." She held him at arm's length, then hugged him, laughing and crying as Jody whined and wagged her tail joyfully.

Rand clutched his mother so tightly he was afraid he hurt her. Ever since he was captured, he'd longed for his ma's gentle touch on his brow. At night when he awoke bathed in sweat from the pain, he had ached to lay his head on her breast and hear her soothing voice as she sang to him. He had been so hurt and bewildered at her silence after his release. Every time the door to the hospital ward opened, he had expected to see her anxious face.

"We thought you were dead."

"I know. There's a lot to tell you. How about some coffee?"

Jacob stopped short when he saw the strange horse munching grass in the shade. "You expecting any-one?" He shot a quizzical look at Shane and his pa.

Jeremiah shook his head. "Looks like that new bay from Larson's Livery. Must be someone from out of town."

They turned their horses over to one of the hands, then headed toward the kitchen door. A low murmur of voices drifted out the screen door, and Jacob paused. It almost sounded like Rand. But he knew better than to fall for that trick of his mind. There were times when he thought he caught a glimpse—out of the corner of his eye—of Rand in his favorite red plaid flannel shirt, striding past. He pushed into the kitchen as a dark-haired man, dressed in a blue Union uniform, rose from the kitchen table and turned to face him.

"Jake."

Rand had coined his nickname, and no one said it quite the way he did. Jacob opened his mouth to question this smiling, dark-eyed stranger who looked like—but of course couldn't be—Rand.

"Rand!" Shane flung himself past Jacob into Rand's waiting arms. A moment later all four men were hugging and slapping one another on the back, unashamed of the tears streaming from their eyes.

"The good Lord answered our prayers after all." With a shaking hand, Pa wiped at his eyes with his bandanna. He was breathing hard, as if he'd just run all the way from the back pasture to the house.

They sat around the kitchen table as Ma hurriedly poured them each a cup of coffee and joined them. Just as she sat down, the front door slammed.

Hannah, the eldest and the only girl, hurried into the kitchen. "Sorry I'm late, Ma." She stopped and looked at the group clustered around the table. Her puzzled stare stopped when her gaze met Rand's. She opened and closed her mouth several times, but no sound escaped.

"What! My gabby sister with nothing to say?" Rand stood, a teasing light in his eyes.

Hannah screamed and dropped the basket she was holding. Potatoes rolled across the wooden floor, and she almost tripped on them as she rushed toward her brother. She threw herself into Rand's arms, and he nearly toppled over.

"Careful," he said. "I'm still not quite myself."

She held him at arm's length. "Explain how this happened."

She hung onto his arm as he limped back to the table and sat down. "I was just about to tell Ma when you so rudely interrupted." He grinned. "Of course, that's nothing new—you've never learned how to be quiet."

"Very funny!" She punched him on the arm and sat beside him.

"Ouch." He rubbed his arm, then turned his grin at his family. "I was captured in northwest Georgia in September of '63. I'd been on reconnaissance, trying to see where the heaviest troop concentrations were. That's how I spent most of the war, slipping back and forth through enemy lines. The Rebs took me to Andersonville prison camp—"

"Andersonville!" Jacob shuddered, remembering the newspaper reports. "That camp is notorious. I heard the Union army found twelve thousand graves there when the war was over. They liberated it last May. You've been free for five months."

Rand nodded. "I was lucky I wasn't one of them. You can't imagine how bad it was. We had to build our own shelters, usually just a lean-to made with whatever we could find. Blankets, clothing, sticks. Some of the men could only dig a hole in the ground and cover up with a thin blanket. There were so many of us we just barely had enough space to lie down. And the food—"

He broke off and took a deep breath. "Well, it wasn't like yours, Ma. We were lucky if they gave us a little salt, maybe a half a cup of beans, and about a cup of unsifted cornmeal. Death was welcome for most of those guys. I helped bury over a hundred bodies in a common grave." His face was white.

Ma laid a trembling hand on his arm. "I just thank God you survived it, son."

He covered her hand with his. "I was delirious by the time we were freed. The doctor said I had dysentery and malnutrition." He smiled grimly. "I weighed less than a hundred pounds when I was brought to the hospital. A skeleton really. I've spent the last five months at Harewood General Hospital in Washington, D.C., recuperating."

"Why didn't you write?" Hannah burst out.

"I did. At least once a month."

Jacob shook his head. "We never received a single letter. Just a notification from the army of your death." He looked at his mother. "You want to show him, Ma?" He felt an inexplicable need to explain their willingness to believe Rand dead.

"I have it right here." Their mother hurried from the room and returned moments later waving a paper.

"See, right here." She thrust it under Rand's nose. "Official notice."

Rand studied it a moment, then handed it back. "There was a lot of confusion in the camps. It's not uncommon for this to happen."

"I knew you weren't dead. I just knew it," Shane put in excitedly. "I told Sarah just last week!"

At the mention of Sarah's name, Jacob's gaze went to his brother. He'd been dreading telling Rand about Sarah. He wouldn't take it well.

Rand stared back at Jacob, his eyes no longer smiling. "What about Sarah, Jake?"

Jacob started, then forced himself to look in his brother's hurt eyes. *He knew.* "What have you heard?"

"I already know she's going to marry Ben Croftner. How could she do that—didn't she mourn me at all?"

"Mourn you? You idiot!" Hannah stood and raked a hand through her mane of chestnut hair. "We all feared for her sanity! She refused to eat for days. Even now she hardly smiles. And you know what a perky, bubbly little thing she always was."

"Then why is she marrying Ben?"

Hannah hesitated, her gaze searching her brother's face. "William is dying." She sat back down beside her brother and took his hand. "Wade has her convinced that marrying Ben will help her father through this tough time. But that wily Ben has promised Wade that fifty acres of prairie he's always coveted as a marriage settlement."

"Hannah, you shouldn't gossip."

"It's not gossip, Ma. Rachel told me. Wade's taken advantage of Sarah's apathy since the news of your death to convince her. She thinks she owes it to the family to do this."

"Wade's always thought of himself instead of his family." Rand's voice was tight. "But there's something else you don't know." He stood and paced over to the window at the front of the kitchen, then wheeled to face them. "Ben has known all along I wasn't dead."

"What!" Their mother stood, her hand on her chest. "Are you sure?"

He nodded grimly. "Ben was with the troops who liberated the prison. I gave him a letter to give to Sarah."

Ma bit her lip. "Maybe he thought you died after he left."

Jacob clenched his fists. He wanted to find Croftner and pummel him. "He knew we read it in the paper last fall. And that we received an official notification shortly after that, I'm positive he never gave Sarah any letter."

"What about all the letters I wrote from the hospital?" Rand sat down and stretched his leg out in front of him.

"Maybe they were lost," Pa said. "The mail service has been wretched."

"All of them?" Rand shook his head. "Not likely. Ben must have gotten hold of them somehow."

"Labe works in the post office."

Shane's announcement silenced everyone. Finally Hannah spoke in a soft, hesitant voice. "Surely Labe wouldn't tamper with the mail." But her tone indicated her own doubt.

Jacob tried to tamp down his anger. "What other explanation is there, Sis?"

Rand got to his feet. "I'm going to see Sarah. Then I'm going to get to the bottom of this."

Ma held out a placating hand. "Let it go for now, son. Try to get a handle on your anger before you talk to Ben."

Rand shook off her hand. "Let it go? After all I've been through, you want me to let it go? Ben needs to find out he can't treat a Campbell like that."

Ma touched Rand's cheek. "What's gotten into you?" She paused, searching his face. "You've always been the even-tempered, rational one in the family."

"What do you expect, Ma? For me to just forget how Ben lied to and deceived the people I love? Well, I just can't do it. Maybe if I hadn't been through so much the last few years, I could. But I thought Ben was my friend. I trusted him. I deserve an explanation for what he's done."

"'Vengeance is mine; I will repay, saith the Lord,'" she quoted softly.

Rand stepped away, shaking his head. Jacob fell into step with him. "I'm going with you."

FOUR

Tomorrow she would be Mrs. Ben Croftner.

Sarah took a sip of tea and tried to drag her attention back to Myra Murphy's conversation, but her thoughts kept whirling around. The last few days had swept by in a daze, and now her future hurtled toward her at breathtaking speed. The lighthearted chatter of her friends around her, the brightly patterned quilt still attached to the quilting frame, the gifts heaped beside her should have brought her joy, but she was numb to all feelings but dread. She didn't want to leave her home, her comfortable, predictable life. And how well did she really know Ben? What if her new life was so different she couldn't adjust?

Suddenly aware of a strange hush in the room, Sarah looked around at the other ladies. They all wore the same look of shock and disbelief. Sarah twisted around to face the door herself to see what could cause such consternation among her friends.

She blinked at the figure blocking the sunlight as his broad shoulders spanned the doorway. Her gaze traveled up the gaunt frame to the face staring back at her intently. She gasped and began to rise to her feet. Was she dreaming? She put a hand to her throat. Her legs felt too weak to support her.

"Sarah."

The voice was so familiar, so beloved. She gasped, then took a step toward him and reached out a trembling hand.

Rand caught her hand. "Hello, Green Eyes." His gaze was as warm as a caress.

Her knees couldn't support her, and she clutched his hand, so warm, so real. She had to be dreaming. Hesitantly she reached up to touch his square jawline.

She felt the rough stubble on his chin. "Rand, it can't be, but it is. You're alive!"

She buried her face against his chest and inhaled his beloved, familiar scent. If it was a dream, she wanted never to awaken. But this was no dream. The rough texture of his uniform under her cheek, the familiar spicy tang of his hair tonic, and most important, the touch of his hands on her waist were all real.

Through a fog, she heard Jacob ask everyone to leave them alone. As soon as the door shut behind them, Rand pulled her away from his chest and she stared up into his brown eyes.

"Where have you been? We thought you were dead!" she whispered, blinking back tears.

"I know you were told I was dead. I stopped home first and Jacob told me." He pulled her back into his arms as if he couldn't bear to let her go.

She nestled against his chest again. This was where she belonged. How had she managed to go on breathing these past months? She sighed and lifted her head. "Tell me what happened."

He explained all the events of the past months while Sarah took in every detail of his appearance. He was too thin, but he looked grand in his blue uniform with the brass buttons gleaming and the cap perched on his dark hair. She shuddered as he described what he'd gone through in prison.

"I was so lost without you."

He stiffened, then picked up her left hand. The engagement ring Ben had given her only days before sparkled in the afternoon sun streaming through the lace curtains. "What about this, Sarah?" He dropped her hand and took a step back. "The thought of you waiting here—loving me, I thought—was the only thing that kept me alive during those long months at Andersonville. The only thing that kept me sane. Now I find you here with another man's ring on your finger."

"But, Rand, it's not what you think." She suddenly realized how bad this had to look to him. She reached toward him and he opened his arms, his expression anguished.

He embraced her for only a moment, then pulled away again. "Sometimes I questioned why I was allowed to live when I saw all my friends die, but I knew it was because you were waiting on me. Depending on me to come back to you. Did our love mean so little to you?"

His voice went hoarse. "I don't know what to think, Sarah."

"We-we thought you were dead," she whispered. "Don't you understand?"

"All I understand is that you forgot me in only a few short months."

"It's not like that. I'll break off the engagement immediately. You have to let me explain how it happened. I don't love him."

He continued to stare at her with a dark sorrow in his eyes. "Your wonderful new fiancé knew all along I wasn't dead."

She shook her head. "No, Rand, he told me—"

He began to pace, his limp becoming more prominent with every step. "He knew, Sarah. I gave him a letter to give to you. Did you get a letter?"

"No, but there must be some mistake. Ben cried when he told me about how he found your body—"

He wheeled around and shook his head. "He lied, Sarah." His voice was soft as if he were trying to make a child understand.

"Bu-but Ben *saw* your body." She felt idiotic repeating herself, but she couldn't seem to reconcile the two totally different stories.

"He was with the troops who liberated the prison, Sarah."

"But we saw in the paper—"

"It was wrong and he knew it was wrong. And how do you explain the letter he neglected to give you? A letter I personally put in his hands." Then he was in front of her, his hands warm on her shoulders. "You said you don't love him. Then why are you marrying him?"

"If I couldn't have you, at least I could make everyone else in my family happy. It seemed noble somehow. Papa wanted me settled before h-he dies. The doctor says he doesn't have long." His breath, so familiar and dear, caressed her face. She reached up and touched the stubble on his face again. "Oh, Rand, this is all too much to take in. I'm sure Ben didn't know."

But a dawning horror spread through her limbs. There were many dark layers to Ben, layers she hadn't wanted to poke into too deeply.

Rand's hands dropped away and he stepped back, his eyes hollow and desperate. "I can't believe you're defending him! I've written you and my folks many times while I was recuperating in Washington. You didn't get any of those letters either. And you know why? Labe works at the post office!" He took off his army hat and raked a hand through his thick hair.

What a fool she'd been. How gullible she was. All that phony sympathy—and the details he'd offered to prove to her Rand was really dead. "But we didn't know!"

Rand took a deep breath. "I didn't expect to have to argue you into believing me. I didn't think you'd defend what he's done. I have to think about this, Sarah." He gave her one last tortured glance before he turned toward to the door and stalked out.

"Rand!" she cried after his retreating figure. "Don't go. I do love you!" She ran after him, but he continued down the porch steps. "Wait. Please, wait." She caught his arm, but he shrugged it off and swung up onto Ranger's back.

He gazed down at her, the muscles in his throat working. "Maybe we can talk again in a few days. I just can't right now." He took a deep breath, then his jaw hardened. He shook his head slightly as though to clear it, dug his heels into the gelding's flank, and turned down the lane.

Jacob stepped from the porch where he'd been waiting and touched her shoulder. "Give him some time, Sarah. It will be all right." He went to his horse and swung into the saddle, then rode after his brother.

She stared after them in horror and disbelief. He had to listen to her—he just had to. She sank onto the porch step and buried her face in her hands. The ring Ben had given her just last week was a little too big, and it scratched her cheek where it had twisted toward her palm. The pain sharpened her senses, and every-thing was heightened. The color of the sky, the scent of autumn in the air. With Rand's reappearance, the numbness encasing her was gone, melted away.

Her senses vibrating, she stared at the ring on her finger. She wrenched it off and threw it as hard as she could toward the woods. She could see it winking in the sunlight as it arced up, then disappeared into the burnished canopy of leaves.

The buckboards and buggies were gone, and the house was quiet when she walked listlessly back inside. The ladies had all discreetly gone home, but the clutter left from the bridal shower was still strewn about the parlor. Rachel had left to go pick up Wade in town. Sarah kicked aside a box and sat down.

She felt numb, drained. There had to be some way to make Rand see, but she was just too tired to find it right now. But at least he was alive. What a wonderful miracle. She curled up on the sofa, her knees drawn up to her chest. She was so very tired. When she woke up she'd think of some way to get through to Rand.

FIVE

Rand paused for a moment on a knoll overlooking the Campbell home sprawling below him. He had so many conflicting emotions. His love for Sarah told him to forgive her and understand the situation, but his overwhelming disappointment just wouldn't let him. Everything was so different than he'd expected. He'd always thought her love was the kind that came along only once in a lifetime. And to find out now that she'd promised to marry Ben while he lay near death was just too much to take in.

"Wait up," Jake said from behind him.

Rand reined in his horse and waited for his brother. "I'm going to town."

"To see Ben?"

"You got it." He wheeled Ranger toward Wabash.

He was reasonably certain where Ben could be found too. Unless he'd changed a lot, he'd be at the back table at the Red Onion. Ben was certainly going to be surprised when Rand walked in. Or maybe not. Maybe he had read his letters before he destroyed them.

They rode silently toward town, the stillness broken only by the clopping of the horses' hooves and the croaking of the frogs along the riverbank. The fecund smell from the river wafted in on the breeze.

"You know where Ben lives?" Rand asked.

"He bought that fancy brick house on Main Street. You know the one Judge Jackson built?"

Rand lifted a brow and glanced at his brother. "How'd he ever afford a place like that?"

"Land speculation, mostly. And investments since he got back, I guess. He's pretty closemouthed about it. I'll show you. If he's not there, we'll head for the Red Onion."

Rand followed his brother as they cantered up the

steep Wabash Street hill and turned down Main Street, dimly illuminated by gaslights. The house loomed over the street, its brick turrets and high peaks grander and more lavish than any of its neighbors.

The men approached the paneled walnut doors, and Rand pounded on the door with his fist, not bothering with the brass knocker. No one answered, and he pounded again.

"I don't think anyone is home," Jacob said.

"We'll catch up with him at the tavern." Rand spun his horse around and cantered for town.

Sarah awoke as the clock chimed, reminding her how late it was. She hurriedly threw more wood into the cookstove and sat at the table to snap green beans. Papa and Joel would be back from town anytime, and Wade, demanding supper, wouldn't be far behind with Rachel. There was a heavy cloud cover, and the smell of rain came through the open window. It was already dark, although it was barely six o'clock.

"Sarah."

She jumped at the sudden sound. She had been

so lost in thought she hadn't heard the knock on the door. Ben had walked into her home as if nothing were amiss. "How dare you come here after what you've done! How could you do such a thing to me—to Rand's family?"

"Rand, always Rand! Don't you care about my feelings at all?" He reached out and swept a vase from the table. His gaze snapped to her bare left hand. "Where's your ring?" He grasped her shoulders and squeezed.

Sarah stared at him. "You think I would marry you after all you've done?" His grip hurt her arms. "After you lied and tricked me? You're not the man I thought you were at all."

Ben ignored her retort. "Where—is—your—ring?" He punctuated every word with a shake, and her hair tumbled out of the pins and down her back.

"I threw it into the woods," she said with a defiant toss of her head.

His fingers bit deeper into the soft flesh of her arms, and she winced. "Do you have any idea how much that ring cost?" he shouted.

"Is money all you care about? Don't you care about the pain you've caused?" She couldn't believe how quickly his tender, well-mannered facade crumbled.

He seized her elbow and yanked her toward the door.

"What are you doing?" Panicked, Sarah tried to free herself. "Let go of me!" The fabric ripped under her elbow as she tried to wrench her arm out of his grip.

"You're mine, Sarah, and no one else's. You're coming with me." He hauled her struggling form through the door and hoisted her up beside Labe, waiting in the buckboard, the brim of his hat pulled low to shield his face from the misty rain just beginning to fall.

Labe's face was pale, and his mouth worked soundlessly. "I'm sorry, Sarah," he finally whispered as he tied her hands together with a piece of rough rope. "I tried to talk him out of this, but there was no stopping him."

"Shut up," his brother snarled as he crawled up beside Sarah. "Everything arranged?"

Labe nodded uncertainly. "Bedrolls are in the back, along with everything else you said."

The glint in Ben's eyes made her gut twist. Was he insane? With renewed fear, she lunged backward, intending to crawl over the bedrolls and out the back, but Ben was too quick for her.

He sat her back in the seat with a bone-jarring thump. "If you don't sit still, I'll truss you up like a chicken."

And he would too. She could see it in his eyes. Shivering from the cold needles of rain that pelted down in earnest now, she huddled in the seat and tried to think of how to get out of this mess.

"You don't need to tie her, Ben." Labe touched her arm, then untied the ropes. "She won't cause no trouble, will you, Sarah?"

She shook her head but couldn't bring herself to lie. She'd jump off this buckboard the moment she could.

Ben picked up the reins, but before he could slap them against the horse's flank, two riders came around the curve of the lane. He squinted in the near darkness. Then his eyes widened.

"Rand!" Sarah cried in relief. She started to clamber over Labe, but Ben grabbed her arm.

"Let go of her, Ben. This is between you and me." Rain dripping from the broad brim of his army hat, Rand slid to the ground and walked toward the buckboard, skirting the widening mud puddles. Jacob followed close behind.

The click as Ben drew back on the hammer of his revolver was muffled in the pattering rain. "Don't come any closer, Campbell."

Rand stopped. "Why'd you do it, Ben? Why lie to everyone?"

Ben's face twisted. "Don't talk to me about lies. You're the biggest liar there ever was." He scoffed. "What a fake. My pa thought the sun rose and set with you. No-account drunk that he was, always getting into scrapes when the liquor got the best of him. I bet you don't even remember the time you stopped and helped him mend our fence and round up the escaped cattle. Like I couldn't have done that if he'd have just asked me. But no, it was always, 'Ben, why can't you be like that Campbell boy?'"

He aimed the gun at Rand. "And then there was Sarah. She mooned over you for years, but did you pay her any notice? No. Even though she was the prettiest girl in Wabash. But just as soon as she took a notice of me, you had to have her. *My* girl."

"I was never your girl!" Sarah's gaze never left his gun.

Ben continued as if he didn't hear her. "When I got back from the war and they all thought you were dead, I knew fate was finally smiling on me. Sarah would be mine. But you had to come back early and spoil everything, just like you always have. Well, you're not going to ruin things for me ever again." He brought the revolver up with sudden determination and fired.

Just as he pulled the trigger, Sarah leaned against him with all her might, and the shot went wild. "Run, Rand!"

But instead of running, Rand launched himself at Ben and dragged him off the buckboard seat. The two men thrashed in the mud and the muck. Rand threw a hard right swing that connected solidly with Ben's cheek. Ben reeled back and hit his head on the wheel of the buckboard as he fell.

Rand pushed his hair out of his eyes and stepped away from Ben. "Is he dead?"

Sarah stared at Ben's pale face and saw him draw a ragged breath. "No." Shivering and soaked to the skin, she climbed awkwardly out of the buckboard on rubbery legs and almost fell as she reached toward Rand. "Thank God you're all right!"

"What were you doing with Ben, Sarah?"

She looked at the scene: a carriage packed as if ready for a journey. She imagined how it must seem to Rand, who'd just learned he'd been deceived on what should have been a happy day of reunion. She stared at him in dismay. Surely he didn't think she was running off with Ben willingly?

She raised her chin. "Ben saw that I'd taken off his ring and dragged me out to the carriage. He'd have kidnapped me if you and Jacob hadn't shown up."

"Is that so?"

She caught his arm again. "Rand, surely you don't believe—"

His eyes hooded, he turned away.

Jacob nudged Ben with his boot. "I think one of us had better ride after Doc Seth. Ben doesn't look too good."

"I'll go." Rand shook off Sarah's restraining hand and mounted his horse. "You keep an eye on Croftner."

She stood looking after him. He had to listen to her eventually. He just had to.

SIX

R and sensed Sarah's gaze on his back as she stood beside Doc Seth, but he resisted looking at her. The rain had soaked through every scrap of his clothing, and he shivered as a buggy came sloshing around the corner. When it stopped, a slight, frail figure slowly clambered down.

"William?"

Sarah's father turned as Rand stepped out from the shadows. Tears started to fill William's eyes as he opened his arms and drew Rand into an embrace. "My dear boy, I heard the news in town. What a happy day this is for all of us."

William had always been frail but vibrant in spite of it all. Rand didn't recognize him in this stoop-shouldered man with deep lines of pain around his mouth. The older man's fragility reminded him of a dying baby bird he'd found once, its bones thin and brittle.

"It-it's good to see you, sir," he stammered, trying to hide his dismay.

"You too, son. You too." William drew back and wiped his eyes shakily with his handkerchief. "What's going on here?"

"I gather that Ben was trying to force Sarah to go off with him." Rand explained Ben's deception.

"This is all so much to take in. When the war ended, it seemed the horrors would at last come to an end. Now it seems they're piling up even in times of peace." William shook his head.

Doc Seth straightened and stepped over to Rand and William. "He'll live, but he's sure going to wake up with a sore head. Labe can take him home and put him to bed, and I'll look in on him tomorrow." He thrust out a hand to Rand. "Good to have you home, young Campbell. Amelia told me the news."

Rand shook his hand. "Tell her I'll stop by and see her soon." He broke off, and they all turned as another horse and buggy cantered into the yard.

Wade slid down from his buggy, his face florid. "What's going on here?" He didn't bother to help his wife down but stomped over to where his father stood.

Joel slid down from the buggy and bounded into Rand's arms. "Rand! Oh, Rand!"

Rand laughed and hugged him tightly. He loved Sarah's little brother as much as his own. "How you doing, half-pint?"

"Great! I've missed you so much. When can we go fishing?"

Rand grinned at the familiar question. He'd always felt sorry for the lad. William's health prevented much of the usual father-son relationship, and Wade wasn't much of a fisherman. He'd started taking Joel fishing when he was two. "Soon."

He pulled a hand free and thrust it out for Sarah's older brother. "Good to see you, Wade." It wasn't really, but he could at least make an attempt at civility.

Wade ignored the outstretched hand. "You beat up my sister's fiancé and think you can just sit on our porch like an old friend? Why aren't you in jail?"

Rand lowered his hand and put it back in his pocket. What was there to say in the face of such animosity? Wade always saw things his own way.

"That's enough!" William's voice boomed out in a sudden surge of strength. "Your treatment of a guest in our home is unacceptable, Wade. You have no idea of the wrong that's been done to him over the past few months."

Wade glared at his father, his massive hands clenched. "So he was a prisoner of war. Lots of men were. He can't just show up here as if we're all going to bow and scrape and give up all we've worked for to accommodate him. Sarah, get inside. We have a wedding to prepare for."

His father lifted a brow. "You know as well as I do that Sarah would never marry Ben now."

Wade's color deepened. "How do you know her feelings haven't changed? Ben would make a much better husband than Campbell."

"Why, because he's rich? A man who could deceive her the way Ben has isn't worthy of my daughter."

William directed a slight smile Sarah's way. "Besides, she loves Rand. Always has, always will. Right, honey?"

Sarah nodded.

The muscles in Wade's jaw pulsed as he clenched his teeth. "But what about the land?"

"Is that all you care about? More land, more money?" William shook his head wearily. "I'm telling you right now, if you do anything to hurt Sarah or Rand, you won't have *this* land or house."

Wade stared at his father. "You'd cut me out of your will?"

"In a minute. Now get in the house until you can get a civil tongue in your head."

Wade shot a glance at Sarah, then swung his blistering gaze toward Rand before stomping into the house. He let the screen door slam shut behind him. Rachel sighed and followed him.

"Good for you, Papa." Sarah slipped her small hand into his.

"Wade's had it coming. I should never have let him get away with his arrogance for so long." William took his hat off and rubbed his forehead. The confrontation had drained him. "Come in out of the rain, sweetheart. You and Rand can have the parlor. I'm just going to have a bite to eat and go to bed." He shook Rand's hand. "Stop by tomorrow and we'll talk. I'm just as eager as Joel to hear the full story." He walked into the house, his shoulders stooped.

Sarah watched her father stumble up the steps and into the house. An order from Pa wouldn't stop Wade for long. Why did he hate Rand so? She shook her head. Ever since she could remember there had been antagonism between them. And Rand had tried. But every overture he'd made had been ignored or ridiculed.

She pushed the disturbing puzzle out of her mind and turned back to Rand. "Can we talk?"

"There's nothing to say right now." His tone was abrupt. "I still don't know how I feel about you or anything else." He took off his sopping hat and ran a weary hand through his wet hair.

"Campbell!" Ben's hoarse growl interrupted them. Glowering, he raised his head from the back of the buckboard. "This isn't over, Campbell. You'll never have her. Never. You just remember that." His head fell back against the floor of the buckboard as Labe slapped the reins against the horse's flank, but Ben watched them until he was out of sight, a burning hatred in his eyes.

Sarah shivered. "I think he means it. Watch your back, Rand."

"I can take care of myself. You're soaked to the bone. You go on in now. Just give me some time."

Sarah hesitated, her eyes searching his sober face. Time? How much time? But she left the questions unanswered and walked wearily up the porch steps, her wet skirt dragging in the mud. She turned to watch Rand and Jacob mount up and ride down the lane and around the curve. Didn't he realize how much time they'd wasted already?

The next morning Rand woke disoriented. The familiar clanging of trays in the hallway and the squeak of nurses' shoes scurrying was missing. Sunshine streamed in the window and illuminated suddenly familiar surroundings. The toy soldiers Grandpa had carved for him when he was five were lined up on a battered chest against the wall. His fingers stroked the brightly colored quilt, soft and faded with numerous washings. The rug on the unpainted wood floor was as threadbare as he remembered it.

He glanced at the space next to him. Jacob was nowhere to be seen, but there was that indentation on the pillow, a sight he'd seen hundreds of times and had thought he'd never see again.

He jumped out of bed, eager to get downstairs. He wouldn't worry about anything today, he decided as he splashed cold water on his face. He was just going to enjoy being with his family again after three long years. No uniform either. He opened his closet, grabbed a pair of overalls and his favorite plaid shirt, and pulled them on. The pants hung around his waist, and they were too long, but they would have to do.

By the time he pulled on socks and boots, the aroma of coffee and ham filled the air and made his stomach rumble. The low murmur of voices quickened his steps as he hurried down the stairs.

His mother spun around as he stepped into the kitchen. "I was just coming to wake you. I fixed ham and eggs, grits, flapjacks, and coffee. I'll have you fattened up in no time." She gave him a quick, reassuring hug.

Rand grinned as he squeezed her, breathing in the faint fragrance of roses that clung to her. She wouldn't be Ma without that scent. He remembered gathering wild roses every summer for her to make sachets for her bureau drawers. He dropped his arms as she bustled over to the cookstove, then offered him a plate piled high with food. His mouth watered as he took it from her and sat between Shane and Jacob.

Hannah came hurrying in as Rand took his first sip of strong, hot coffee. Her face brightened as she saw Rand shoveling another forkful of eggs into his mouth. "Now I am sure it's really you." She slipped into the chair opposite him. "The brother I remember is always eating."

Rand, a wicked grin on his face, caught Jacob's eye and gave a meaningful nod. "How come you're still here, anyway, Sis? Thought you would have trapped yourself a husband by now."

"Come on, Rand. Be realistic." Jacob poked him with an elbow. "Who would have her? She has always been the ugliest Campbell."

Rand stared at his sister. "Yeah, I forgot about that big nose of hers. And all that hair."

"Not to mention her temper! Her tongue could cut a man to ribbons." Jacob grinned at the rising color on Hannah's face.

Rand knew they'd get a reaction when they hit on her sore spot. She was always moaning about her nose. Personally, Rand didn't see anything wrong with it, but she seemed to think it didn't match the pert ones described in her favorite novels.

She flushed a deep red, then burst into tears.

"Hey, I'm sorry, Sis." Rand hadn't expected this much of a reaction. He reached over and put an arm around her. "You know we were only teasing. I've always liked your nose."

Hannah just cried harder. "It's not that," she finally sputtered as Rand handed her his bandanna. She drew a deep breath. "It's just so wonderful to have you here, to see Jacob smile again, to hear your voice—" She stopped and gulped.

The dimples deepened in Rand's cheeks as he stared at his sister. "It sure is good to be home. To be with you all again just like before this crazy war ever happened. You don't know how anxious I was to get home. I was so scared when no one answered my letters."

Their parents had been watching the exchange between their children with indulgent smiles, and Ma's eyes welled with tears at Rand's words. She dabbed at her eyes with a lace-edged hankie.

His dad cleared his throat gruffly. "You're just in time to help with the farming too. It's almost more than Shane and I can handle. I've tried to talk your brother into staying home, but he won't listen. Now I'll have some help come spring."

Rand glanced at Jacob. Hadn't he told them of Rand's plans? He and his brother had lain awake for hours talking last night. He'd been hoping that by now Jacob would have broken the news to their father. His brother shook his head slightly.

Pa's gaze traveled from one son to the other. "What is it?"

Rand hated to disappoint their father. "I-I won't be able to stay long, Pa," he stammered. "I'm in the Third Cavalry. I can stay for about a week, but then I have to report for duty." He winced at the stricken look in his mother's eyes. "I've been garrisoned at Fort Laramie. I still have two years to go of my service."

"Not you too!" Hannah stood twisting her hands in her apron. "The Sioux have been rampaging for months out there. Isn't it bad enough we're losing Jacob?"

Jacob shrugged. "That's why so many of us are being sent out West. And I've found out in the past couple of years how much I enjoy the cavalry. I've always wanted to see the frontier, so I don't mind the assignment. Maybe I can find my own spread while I serve my country."

"Rand, no." His father rose to his feet. "Why do you think I've worked so hard on this farm? Always expanding, always looking for ways to make more money?" He put an arm around Ma. "It's been for you! For you and your brothers. You can't go! Surely the army would release you after all you've been through."

His mother flinched as the words echoed in the warm kitchen. He stood and faced his father. "I don't want to be released. I'm a grown man, Pa. This is what I want."

Ma laid a gentle hand on his arm. "Your pa is just concerned, Rand. Can't you think about staying home now and letting us all begin to heal? You can raise horses right here on land that's been in the Campbell family for twenty-five years instead of fighting Indians to gain a small piece of land in some godforsaken wilderness. You haven't been with us for three years."

His mother had always been able to change his mind in the past, and he fought against the soft persuasion in her voice. "I can't, Ma." He raked a hand through his hair. "I need to prove something to myself, to build my own dreams with my own sweat. I have to go."

Pa took a long look at his son's granite face, then left the room. Ma opened her mouth to try again, but one look at the firm set to Rand's mouth changed her mind.

Always the peacemaker, Hannah cleared her throat and laughed self-consciously. "So, the calvary, huh? You've always had the magic touch with horses and cattle. When Ma was carrying Jacob, she asked you if you wanted a baby brother or sister. You looked up with those brown eyes of yours all serious and said, 'If it's all the same to you, Ma, I'd just as soon have a horse.'"

Laughter defused the tension as they heard the familiar story. Jacob punched Rand in the arm. "Yeah, and you've been treating me like a beast of burden ever since!"

When the laughter faded, Hannah looked at Rand and said softly, "You are taking Sarah, aren't you?"

Rand looked away from her expectant face. "No." It was all he could do to shake his head, to stick to his decision. "Not right now. I need some time to accept all that's happened. I'll keep in touch, and down the road, we'll see if we can work things out." He folded his arms across his chest. "Anyway, that area is no place for a woman. She'd soon get sick of being confined to the fort. You know how independent she is."

"Jacob is taking Amelia. It must not be too dangerous."

Hannah's expression turned mutinous as she opened her mouth to argue further.

"Don't push me, Hannah. I know you're concerned, but I have to be sure in my own mind why she took up with Ben. She was mighty young when I left for the war—only sixteen. I need to be sure she knows her own mind."

Hannah sighed impatiently. "Why are men so thickheaded?" She rolled her eyes.

Rand grinned and pushed away from the table. "It's the only protection we have against you women." He stood and stretched. "Better get to the fields. I'll help all I can while I'm here."

"What about your leg?"

"I feel fine, Sis. And I need to work at getting my strength back." He grabbed his hat and followed his brothers out the door.

Out on the porch, Jacob stopped and thrust his

hands in his pockets. "Don't you know how rare it is to find someone to love the way you love Sarah? Don't throw it away."

Rand looked away. "Nothing was like I expected, Jake. Things turned out pretty well for you, though. You and Amelia. You'll be married and off on an adventure together."

"You could be, too, if you weren't so pigheaded." Jacob's lips flattened, then finally curved into a smile. "Swallow your pride. Go see Sarah. She never stopped loving you. She pined for you. Haven't you even noticed how thin she is? If losing you once nearly destroyed her, what do you think losing you again would do to her? You'll come back and find her dead and buried."

Rand inhaled sharply at the thought. He stared into his brother's brown eyes and saw the certainty there. "It wouldn't hurt to just talk, I reckon."

Jacob clapped his hand on Rand's shoulder. "Then get to it. I can handle the plowing."

Sarah sighed as she stared across the river. What could she do to change Rand's mind? She hadn't heard a word from him all day. Should she try to find him? But he'd said to give him some time. So she'd come to their favorite spot to wait him out. She leaned down and picked up a flat rock. She skimmed it across the water, and it skipped three times. Not very good. She was losing her touch. She reached down for another rock.

"The last time I saw you do that, it skipped six times."

She turned immediately and smiled. Rand. It was almost as if her hopeless wishing had conjured him up. "Oh, Rand, I'm so glad you came."

He held out his arms, and she rushed into them. The scent of his hair tonic slipped up her nose. A familiar scent that clouded her thoughts into a hopeless jumble.

She buried her face in his broad chest and clung until he lifted her chin. His brown eyes searched her face, and the touch of his breath on her cheek was like a caress. She'd waited so long for this. His mouth came down on hers, so tentative yet so familiar. As his lips touched hers, she wrapped her arms around his neck and kissed him back with all the love in her heart.

He pulled her closer, his right hand pressing her

waist. His passionate response convinced her she hadn't lost him after all. It would be all right. It had to be.

"I tried to stay away, Green Eyes, but I couldn't," he whispered. He loosed his grip on her with a sigh.

She refused to step away and clung to his shirt with both hands. "I'm so sorry about Ben." How did she even begin to explain?

"It's not your fault." He shook his head. "I realized it as soon as I cooled down enough to think. I can't blame you for wanting to go on with your life."

"You are my life. Nothing seemed real with you gone. I-I knew I couldn't be happy, so I thought if everyone else was happy, it would be enough." She swallowed hard, remembering the hopelessness of her future. "But I dreaded the very thought of marriage." She looked up at him.

"You're that opposed to marrying?" His dimple flashed.

The pressure in her chest increased. "Not to marrying the right man."

"And who would that be?" His voice held a teasing lilt she hadn't heard in so long.

"I think you know." The joy she felt inside almost couldn't be contained. "James Benson left on the wagon train last May, and his cabin is still empty. We can live there until our place is built on our knoll."

Rand's smile faded and he looked away. "I can't stay, Sarah. I'm still in the cavalry. I'm heading out West in a couple of days."

She inhaled and held her breath as his words soaked in. "Not staying here?" She stared at him. "But we've always planned to build on the knoll and help Papa with the farm. He's not well, Rand. I can't go running off out West and leave him. Besides, where else would we go?"

"I'm going West." He reached out and wrapped a strand of her hair around his finger. "Your pa will understand. He came here with your ma and settled just like I want to do. He wasn't content to stay in Philadelphia."

The very thought filled her with terror. "That was different. He was poor and had no prospects. You have land here, both mine and yours from your pa. Can't you ask to be released so you can heal?" She wanted to grab him and shake some sense into him. "Surely you're not serious about this scheme. We've made too many other plans."

"It's not different. Once my enlistment's over,

I don't want to take something another man built. There's so much opportunity out West, Sarah. Land for the taking, gold, new businesses." His dark eyes glowed, and he gripped her shoulders in his big hands. "It will be a great life. Besides, do you really think Wade and I could get along well enough to work together?"

"Rand." Panic stole her breath. "I couldn't leave Papa. You haven't seen how ill he's been. He seems to go downhill every day. It would kill him for me to leave."

He frowned. "I saw how poorly he looked. But Sarah, he would understand. He wouldn't want you to stop living because of him. Let's go ask him." He took her arm and started toward the house, but she pulled away.

"No! I don't want to upset him. I just can't go now. Can't you wait? Just until he doesn't need me? He doesn't have very long. The doctor said maybe a year."

"I have my orders and a letter to deliver for General Sherman. I have to go."

She took a deep breath and stepped back from him. "You can't ask me to sacrifice my father." Tears filled her eyes as she saw Rand's face fall. She *couldn't* leave Papa.

"I understand. I love your father too. Good-bye, Sarah. Have a good life." He turned and left her standing on the path.

She opened her mouth to call him back, but the words died in her throat. What was the use? She couldn't go and he wouldn't stay. It was as simple as that. He didn't really love her, or he wouldn't ask her to leave Papa. Not as sick as he was. Couldn't Rand see that? She grabbed a flat stone and hurled it toward the water. It skipped seven times and sank. But there was no one left to see.

ONE

September 22, 1865

The town of Wabash, Indiana, bustled with activity as the horse's hooves clopped along the plank street and up the hill. Rand Campbell reined in the mare pulling the family buckboard and stopped in front of the train depot. The engine shrieked and puffed out a billow of soot that burned his throat as he, Jacob, and Shane climbed down. Now that the time had arrived for his departure, Rand wished he had been able to stay longer. Leaving his mother and father had been rough. Ma had cried, then pressed his grandma's Bible into his hand before hurrying away, and Pa wouldn't even come out of the barn to say good-bye.

Shane snuffled, and Rand ruffled his brother's blond hair, then hugged him. "I'm counting on you to take care of the family, squirt." Though at fifteen, the lad was eye level with Rand.

Shane bit his quivering lip and nodded, straightening his shoulders. He trotted around behind the buckboard, heaved the saddle over one shoulder, then led Ranger to the waiting train. Rand's horse would accompany him west.

Rand put his hand in his pocket. His fingers rubbed against a familiar round shape. He'd smuggled it into the prison in his shoe and had spent months sanding off the engraving on the golden eagle coin before chiseling his and Sarah's names into the gold.

His gaze swept the familiar sights of Wabash at the top of the hill. The whitewashed courthouse, the jail to the west of it, and the bustle of Commercial Row just down the steep Wabash Street hill made his heart ache at the thought of leaving. But knowing he'd never see Sarah again hurt the most.

He'd come home after his internment in Andersonville Prison to find his fiancée engaged to Ben Croftner. When things were sorted out and Ben's lies were exposed, Rand had hoped Sarah would go west with him, but she'd put her family above him. He'd taken that hurt and used it to build a wall around his heart.

He fingered the love token. What good would it do in his pocket? He'd never give it to anyone else because he'd never feel like this about anyone else. That kind of love was dead for him.

He pulled out the token and thrust it into Jacob's hand. "Give this to Sarah, Jake. Tell her I'm sorry it didn't work out and I hope she has a happy life."

Jacob's fingers closed around the token. "You make it sound like there's no hope for the two of you."

"There isn't. I wish it weren't so, but I doubt I'll see Sarah again." Rand hefted the haversack over his shoulder and picked up the hamper of food, then his satchel.

"All aboard!"

He was a cavalry man, and this was what he wanted—a life he made for himself, beholden to no one. After one last look at his brothers, he raced toward the plodding train and jumped up the steep steps. He caught one last glimpse of Jacob, standing with one arm upraised, his other arm around their younger brother, Shane. Rand waved until the buckboard with the two figures beside it was no longer in view, then took a deep breath and limped to a vacant seat. His great adventure was about to begin.

Sarah Montgomery sat on a rock along the banks of the Wabash River and listened to the train whistle blow as the engine left the station. The sun on this fine September day warmed her face. A robin, its red breast a bright flash of color, fluttered by to land on a nearby gooseberry bush. The bird swooped down to grab a worm. The rhythm of life went on even though her heart felt dead in her chest. She was only nineteen, but right now she felt like ninety.

How did she go on after losing Rand and then finding him again, only to watch him leave her without a thought? Time stretched in front of her, a lifetime spent without the man she'd loved since she was a girl.

A vision of his dark hair and eyes resided in her heart and always would.

She picked up the book she'd brought with her, *A Christmas Carol*. The novel absorbed her until the sun moved lower in the sky. She closed it and glanced around to make sure she had all her belongings before going back to the house to start dinner.

"Sarah?"

She looked up to see Jacob, Rand's younger brother, approaching with a tentative smile. "He's gone?"

Jacob, dressed in his blue cavalry uniform, took off his wide-brimmed hat and turned it in his hands. "I'm sorry, Sarah. How you doing?"

Though her eyes burned, she was past tears. "I'll be fine." She tipped up her chin. "I have Papa and Joel to care for." She studied the compassion in Jacob's brown eyes. "D-Did he say anything about me?"

Jacob nodded and stepped closer. He pulled his hand from his pocket and something metallic winked in the sunlight. "He asked me to give you this."

She rose from her perch on a rock and reached out to take it from him. Her fingers rubbed over the gold metal. "A love token." She choked out the words as she stared at the words engraved in the metal. *Rand and Sarah.*

"He worked on this in prison."

Her fingers traced the engraving. "Did he say anything about me joining him?"

Jacob's eyes held sympathy as he shook his head. "No, he didn't, Sarah. I'm sorry. H-He said to tell you he was sorry it didn't work out and he hoped you'd have a happy life."

The pain crushed in on her again. The good-bye was final, just like the one that loomed with her father. Her fingers closed around the coin, and the edges bit into her palm. "Thank you, Jacob. I'll treasure it."

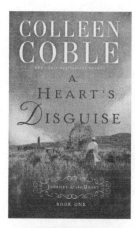
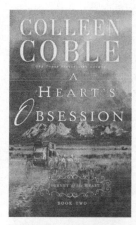
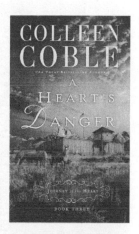
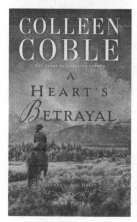
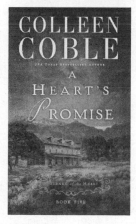
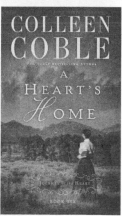

ESCAPE TO BLUEBIRD RANCH

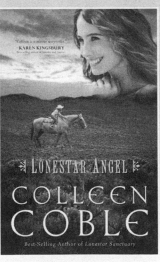

AVAILABLE IN PRINT AND E-BOOK

"*The Lightkeeper's Bride* is a wonderful story filled with mystery, intrigue, and romance. I loved every minute of it."

— CINDY WOODSMALL —
New York Times best-selling author of *The Hope of Refuge*

THE BEST-SELLING MERCY FALLS SERIES.

ALSO AVAILABLE IN E-BOOK FORMAT

THOMAS NELSON
Since 1798

A VACATION TO SUNSET COVE WAS HER WAY OF
celebrating and thanking her parents. After all,
Claire Dellamore's childhood was like a fairytale.
But with the help of Luke Elwell, Claire discovers
that fairytale was really an elaborate lie . . .

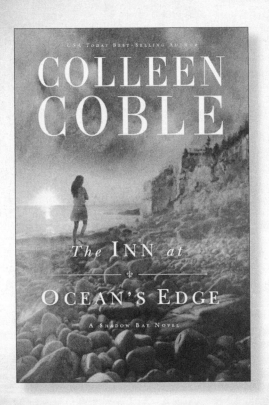

THE FIRST SUNSET COVE NOVEL

AVAILABLE APRIL 2015

THOMAS NELSON
Since 1798

COLLEEN LOVES TO HEAR FROM HER READERS!

Be sure to sign up for Colleen's newsletter for insider information on deals and appearances.

Visit her website at www.colleencoble.com
Twitter: @colleencoble
Facebook: colleencoblebooks

About the Author

Photo by Clik Chick Photography

RITA finalist Colleen Coble is the author of several bestselling romantic suspense novels, including *Tidewater Inn*, and the Mercy Falls, Lonestar, and Rock Harbor series.